Licensed exclusively to Top That Publishing Ltd
Tide Mill Way, Woodbridge, Suffolk, IP12 1AP, UK
www.topthatpublishing.com
Copyright © 2016 Tide Mill Media
All rights reserved
0 2 4 6 8 9 7 5 3 1
Manufactured in China

Written by Oakley Graham
Illustrated by Olive May Green

ISBN 978-1-78445-305-3

A catalogue record for this book is available from the British Library

A holiday ADVENTURE

Illustrated by
Olive May Green

Written by
Oakley Graham

Panda, **Fox** and **Donkey** are the very best of friends! They love to travel and enjoy meeting new people and discovering new places.

The friends were on holiday in **California**, in **North America**, and decided to go on a camping trip. They were so excited that they left their map behind, and they were soon completely …

Panda, Fox and Donkey drove all through the day and all through the night, and for five more days after that ... until they arrived at a busy city with enormous skyscrapers. They had driven all the way to **New York City!**

That evening they watched a music show on Broadway and ate yummy hot dogs in Times Square.

The next day, the three friends reached a port. They drove the camper van on to a gigantic boat which sailed across the Atlantic Ocean to **Europe**.

The boat took them all the way to **England!** Panda, Fox and Donkey decided that it would be rude if they didn't visit the Queen in **London**.

So that's exactly what they did!

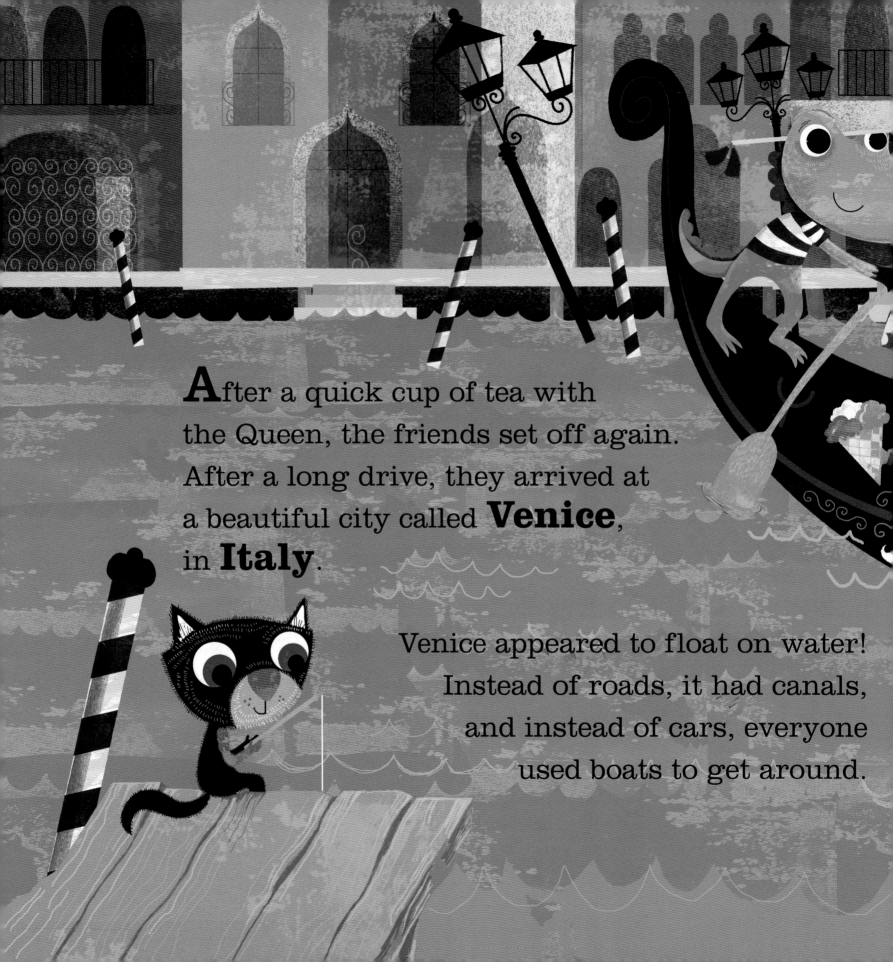

After a quick cup of tea with
the Queen, the friends set off again.
After a long drive, they arrived at
a beautiful city called **Venice**,
in **Italy**.

Venice appeared to float on water!
Instead of roads, it had canals,
and instead of cars, everyone
used boats to get around.

That evening, Panda, Fox
and Donkey travelled in a
gondola to a fancy-dress ball.
It was lots of fun being lost!

The next day, the three friends travelled south, crossing the Mediterranean Sea. They drove through vast deserts, bustling old towns and past huge waterfalls, but their campsite was still nowhere to be seen. They were in **Africa!**

There were lots of amazing things to see in Africa, but the friends liked going on safari in **Kenya** the best.

From Kenya, the friends took a cargo ship across the Indian Ocean to a place called **Australia**. Australia was amazing! The friends snorkelled at the Great Barrier Reef …

… looked at some amazing cave paintings in wild regions called 'the outback' …

... and had barbecues with new friends on the beach.

Still determined to find their campsite, the friends island-hopped all the way to **Asia**. When they reached **China**, Panda visited her family, and Fox and Donkey had great fun playing with dragon kites. As Fox played with his kite, Donkey noticed something sticking out of his jumper – it was the map! The three friends had travelled right around the world, and the map had been with them all along!

Looking at the map, the friends could see where they were supposed to be camping! 'Look at all the places we've visited,' said Donkey.
'Yes, but look at all the wonderful places we haven't been to,' replied Panda.
'I think we should keep exploring,' suggested Fox.

The friends all agreed that travelling around the world had been the best holiday adventure ever! 'Next stop **South America!**' said Panda, as they set off on their learning journey once more.